To Pippa Gerrett and Year Four (2004)
of Sturminster Marshall First School,
where this story began – JJ

For Suzy – with love LC

by Julia Jarman and Lynne Chapman

First published in 2007 by Hodder Children's Books
First published in paperback in 2008

Text copyright © Julia Jarman 2007
Illustration copyright © Lynne Chapman 2007

Hodder Children's Books
338 Euston Road
London NW1 3BH

Hodder Children's Books Australia
Level 17/207 Kent Street
Sydney, NSW 2000

The right of Julia Jarman to be identified
as the author and Lynne Chapman as the illustrator
of this Work has been asserted by them in accordance
with the Copyright, Designs and Patents Act 1988.

A catalogue record of this book is
available from the British Library.

ISBN: 978 0 340 91161 7
10 9 8

Printed in China

Hodder Children's Books
is a division of Hachette
Children's Books.
An Hachette UK Company
www.hachette.co.uk

www.juliajarman.com
www.lynnechapman.co.uk

CLASS TWO AT THE ZOO

JULIA JARMAN

Illustrated by
LYNNE CHAPMAN

Hodder Children's Books

A division of Hachette Children's Books

On the day Class Two went to the zoo,
they saw a koala kissing a kangaroo.

...the anaconda. zzzz

They heard Teacher say,
'We must keep together!'
'Don't wander off!' and
'Watch the weather!'

They saw parrots
squabbling in the sky,
but they didn't see...

...the anaconda sigh, and open one eye to spy on Class Two as they walked round the zoo.

They saw hippos **hopping** in the mud.

They saw monkeys eating **chocolate pud.**

But they didn't see

the anaconda

ponder...

...then **slide** from the water
and start to wander...

...after Class Two
on their trip round the zoo,
some of them walking two by two.

They saw spotty cheetahs
running a mile.

They saw
two gorillas
jumPing
a stile.

But they failed to see that **huge** reptile...

...Open his jaws and swallow Kyle.

They didn't see that **giant** snake...

...add **Diana** to his feast.

MONKEYS LEMURS PENGUINS

...gulp down **Gerty and Anita.**

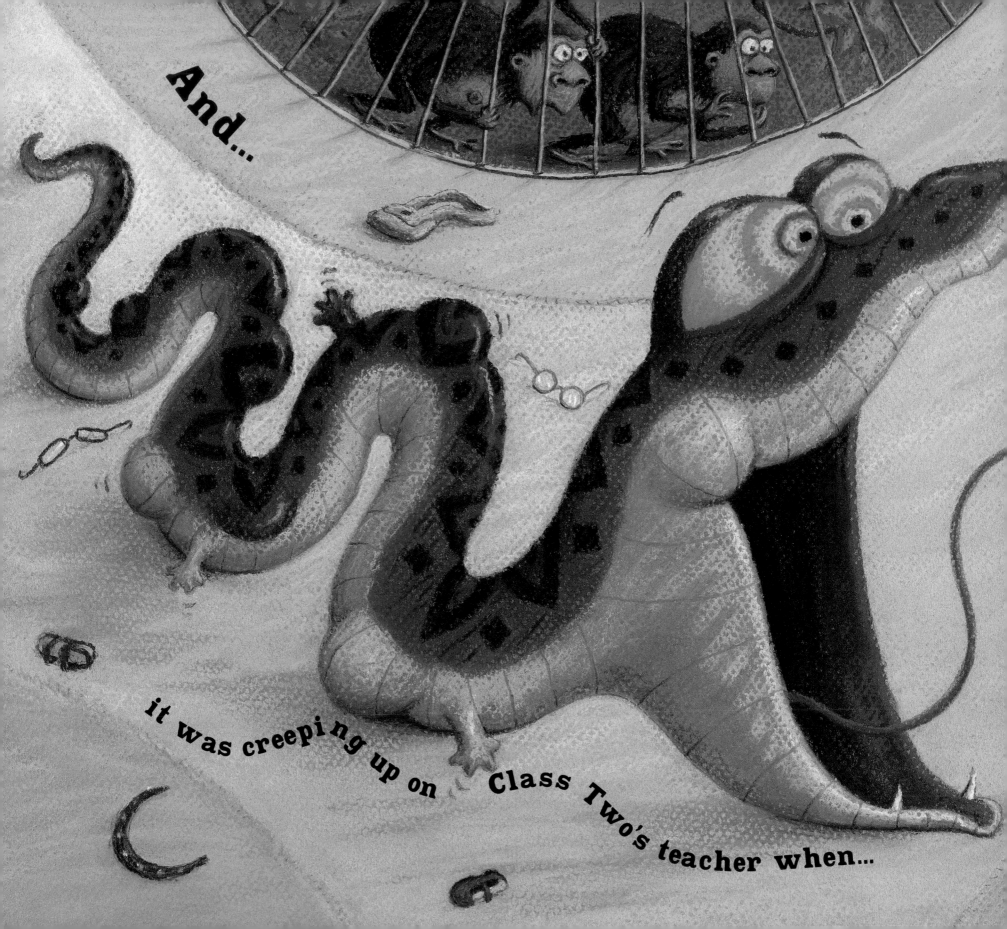

And...

it was creeping up on   Class Two's teacher when...

Molly turned and saw **the creature!**

Well, most of **Kate** – so **Molly** was quick.

She grabbed hold of a sturdy stick.

Without a single moment's pause she stuck it between the **monster's jaws.**

'Come on!' she urged the rest of Class Two – as she grabbed Kate's feet – **'To the rescue!'**

The rest of Class Two all heaved and tugged...

and Gerty...

and Diana...

and Anita,

and Jake,

and James...

and Kyle –

his smile
as wide as
a crocodile!

Then a boy they didn't know.

'Thank you,' he said,

'my name is Joe.'

'Phew!' said Class Two as they fled from the zoo.

Let this be a terrible warning for you!

When you go on a safari or visit a zoo,
keep your eyes open whatever you do.

Watch out for the snake,
lying low in the lake,
and if you see the anaconda
open an eye and start to wander,
don't, even for a second, ponder...

run!